엄마 마중
WAITING FOR MAMA

A Bilingual Picture Book

이태준 글   by LEE Tae-Jun
김동성 그림   Illustrated by
KIM Dong-Seong

Text copyright © 1938 by Lee, Tae-Jun
Illustrations copyright © 2004 by Kim, Dong-Seong
All rights reserved.
Original Korean edition published by Sonyunhangil,
an imprint of Hangilsa Publishing Co., Ltd. through Shinwon Agency Co.
First published in Korea under the title 엄마 마중.

Copyright © 2007 by Baobab, an imprint of NordSüd Verlag AG, Zürich,
Switzerland. Publisher: Kinderbuchfonds Baobab, Basel, Switzerland.
Published in Switzerland under the title *Wann kommt Mama?*
English translation copyright © 2007 by North-South Books Inc., New York.

First published in the United States and Canada in 2007 by North-South
Books Inc., an imprint of NordSüd Verlag AG, Zürich, Switzerland.
Distributed in the United States by North-South Books Inc., New York.

Library of Congress Cataloging-in-Publication Data is available.
A CIP catalogue record for this book is available from The British Library.

ISBN-13: 978-0-7358-2143-9 / ISBN-10: 0-7358-2143-7 (trade edition)
10 9 8 7 6 5 4 3 2 1

Printed in Belgium

www.northsouth.com

엄마 마중
WAITING FOR MAMA

A Bilingual Picture Book

이태준 글   by LEE Tae-Jun
김동성 그림   Illustrated by
KIM Dong-Seong

Translated from
Korean to English by
Eun Hee Chun

Afterword by
Andreas Schirmer

NORTHSOUTH
BOOKS

NEW YORK

추워서 코가 새빨간 아가가 아장아장 전차 정류장으로 걸어 나왔습니다.

A small child, his nose red from cold, walks to the streetcar station.

그리고 '낑' 하고 안전 지대에 올라섰습니다.

He climbs up on the high platform.

이내 전차가 왔습니다. 아가는 갸웃하고 차장더러 물었습니다.

Soon a streetcar pulls in. The child peeks in and asks the driver:

"우리 엄마 안 와요?"
"Isn't my mama coming?"

"너희 엄마를 내가 아니?" 하고 차장은 '땡땡' 하면서 지나갔습니다.

"Do I know your mama?" asks the driver, and he drives off, ringing the bell. *Ding-ding!*

또 전차가 왔습니다. 아가는 또 갸웃하고 차장더러 물었습니다.

Another streetcar comes along. Again, the child peeks in and asks the driver:

"우리 엄마 안 와요?"
"Isn't my mama coming?"

"너희 엄마를 내가 아니?" 하고 이 차장도 '땡땡' 하면서 지나갔습니다.

"Do I know your mama?" asks the driver. And he too drives off, ringing the bell.
Ding-ding! Ding-ding!

그 다음 전차가 또 왔습니다. 아가는 또 갸웃하고 차장더러 물었습니다.

The next streetcar comes along. Again the child peeks in and asks the driver:

"우리 엄마 안 와요?"

"Isn't my mama coming?"

"오! 엄마를 기다리는 아가구나." 하고 이번 차장은 내려와서,

"Oh, are you waiting for your mama?" asks the driver, getting off the streetcar.

"다칠라. 너희 엄마 오시도록 한군데만 가만히 섰거라, 응?" 하고 갔습니다.

"You will get hurt standing so close," says the driver. "Stand still over here until your mama comes, okay?" And he drives away.

아가는 바람이 불어도 꼼짝 안 하고,

The child stands still, even though the wind
blows hard.

전차가 와도 다시는 묻지도 않고,

The child doesn't ask any questions, even
when the next streetcar comes.

코만 새빨개서 가만히 서 있습니다.

He just stands there, patiently, with his cold, red nose.

Afterword

The author of this story, Lee Tae-Jun, was born in 1904. He was just 21 years old when he published his first work. He worked as an author until his death in North Korea in 1956. Today, he is still one of Korea's most beloved authors. This story, *Waiting for Mama*, first appeared in a newspaper in 1938.

The illustrator, Kim Dong-Seong, was born in 1970. In this book, he drew the people and scenery as they might have looked in 1938. Even today, in Seoul, you can still see people dressed in these traditional clothes. It is also quite common to see Koreans sitting comfortably on their heels, the way you see people sitting at the streetcar station in this book. Women often carry babies by strapping them onto their backs with wide strips of fabric. Handcarts and old black bikes towering with packages are also still prevalent. Many old women still believe that the best way to carry a package—even a fragile one—is to balance it on your head. In the mountains, you might still see a man with a heavily loaded wooden-framed contraption on his back, with a stick in each hand to keep his balance. Seoul's streetcars are gone now. They disappeared in the last 40 years, having been replaced with subways.

The Writing of the King

Seventy million people live on the Korean peninsula, which includes North and South Korea. There are also many Koreans living in Japan, China, Russia, the United States, Canada, and many other countries. There are approximately 80 million native speakers of Korean worldwide.

Those who speak Korean use the Korean writing called Hangeul. Hangeul is written as 한글 and pronounced **hahng**-gool. Hangeul is the official Korean alphabet. It is a unique script that was created more than 560 years ago under Korea's King Sejong. Before King Sejong, Koreans used Chinese characters for their written language. Written Chinese was only accessible to educated members of society, as it is not phonetic, so many Koreans were frustrated by not being able to write their own language. King Sejong set up a school inside the palace and hired scholars to create a new written language for his people.

The goal of the new written Korean language was to create a language made for Korean speakers. It would be easy enough that anyone could learn it. Since the new writing was based on a phonetic system, it could even duplicate sounds from nature: wind blowing, cranes calling, or dogs barking. The scholars were especially proud of this particular quality of their new written language.

Today, all Koreans use Hangeul for writing, and you see it in this book. Hangeul has fourteen consonants and ten vowels. That's about the same as the English alphabet. If you look at the way the word "Hangeul" is written, you'll notice that Koreans do not write letters in a line the way we write in English. Instead, letters get stacked in squares, like this 한글 .If you were to break down the square that spells Hangeul, and write the letters next to each other, it would look like this: ㅎ (h) ㅏ (a) ㄴ (n) ㄱ (g) ㅡ (eu) ㄹ (l). Syllables are always put together, which makes the Korean language very practical. King Sejong's scholars planned their written language very carefully indeed.

Andreas Schirmer
Translated by Marianne Martens